Contents

1 The Bears

My name is Papa Bear and I live with
my family – Mama Bear and Baby Bear –
in a little house on the edge of the forest.
I'm a taster in the local honey factory.

It was a great day in my life when I
was made Chief Honey Taster. This
means I have to taste every pot before it
can leave the factory. As a result I'm
putting on weight and my fingers are
always sticky. But I love my job.

Usually when I get home Mama Bear has my chair drawn up by the fire and my slippers out. I go up and say 'goodnight' to Baby Bear who has just gone to bed and then my supper is on the table.

We are a very happy family.

But one night when I got home, the place was in a mess. Flour all over the floor, milk spilt, Mama looking cross and Baby Bear sitting on the floor howling.

I stared, in total shock.

'What's up?' I gasped.

'It's that son of yours,' snapped Mama Bear. 'He's a handful. I can't look after him *and* the house *and* cook *and* shop.'

'But you've always done it.'

'BB is getting bigger – have you looked at him lately? – and he's much more trouble. We must get an *au pair*.'

'A what?'

'An *au pair*. It's what they call baby-sitters these days.'

'But...' I began, thinking of the cost.

'No "buts". Put an ad in **at once**... and now help me clear up this mess.'

I argued with her of course, but she insisted. We had to have an *au pair*.

Anyway, to make a long story short, I put an ad into *The Daily Howl.*

'Au Pair wanted for one of the best homes in the county. One small and well-behaved bear. Healthy home cooking. Good wages for the right girl. Apply by phone.'

'Thirty words!' said the dope at the other end. 'That'll cost you! And you can't specify girl or boy. Sexist.'

I cut it down and of course she made a mess of it. It ended up: 'Au pair wanted county home. Small beer ("bear"). Some ("home") cooking. Wages. Apply –'

7

The first *au pair* was a disaster. Yak, yak, yak, from morning to night and I don't think she knew a thing about kids. She disappeared after three days.

But that was not the end of her. She lugged her old Pa around to threaten us and he said they were going to have us up before the Tribunal for Unfair Dismissal! I had to give them a few euro to get rid of them.

I think they did this for a living.

Then Mary Mary Quite Contrary applied. I hoped she would fill the bill.

She didn't talk. She sang. From dawn until midnight.

At the crack of dawn she was warbling *If you ever come to Ireland* and she had hardly seen *the sun go down on Galway Bay* than she was asking *How can you buy Killarney?* When I came home I was greeted by *The Darling Girl from Clare* before climbing *The Hills of Donegal.* Then it was off with *The Bard of Armagh* to *The Mountains of Mourne.* I went to sleep to the news that *It's a long, long way to Tipperary.* (As if I didn't know).

She just never stopped – we must have
been the only people who didn't tell her
to put a sock in it, *ie:* shut up.

Mama Bear said it was 'cultural' for
Baby Bear and I must say he loved it all.
He trailed around after her lisping *Oh,
the Days of the Kerry Dances* and doing
some class of a jig, but I wondered
would my ear-drums last the pace.

She left after five days. She decided her career was in singing, not child care. No wonder they called her 'contrary'!

I wanted to drop the whole idea but Mama Bear dug her heels in.

Just as we were in despair, Goldilocks showed up. And was she well primed!

'I've heard *so* much about you, Papa and Mama Bear,' she said, shyly offering a bunch of flowers. 'And this little dote,' (he was trying to kick her – he wanted Mary Mary back) 'must be Baby Bear. And what a *quaint* little house.'

'Just think,' said Mama Bear, 'she has a letter from the King and Queen. She used to work in the Royal Nursery.'

She was barely able to talk she was so excited. 'Think of how it will look to the nasty Wilde-Bores when they hear the Royal babysitter is working for us.'

'That girl could be an axe murderer,' I told her. But she didn't care. The truth is that Mama Bear never listens to me.

She just makes up her own mind.

2 Goldilocks

Goldilocks was to move in next day, the day the circus came to town.

We took Little Bear to the parade and was he excited! His eyes were agog as the lions, the tigers, the ponies, the knife-throwers and the fire-eaters went by.

When we got home, Goldilocks was sitting on the steps, in tears.

'I thought you were never coming back,' she wept, 'and that I would be left all alone in the world.'

'You poor dear,' said Mama Bear. 'Come right in and have a nice cup of tea … Papa, look after her luggage.'

The taximan was still unloading it.

She had ten cases! I picked up one. It was as heavy as lead.

'You'll have to help me,' I said to the taximan. 'I have a bad back.'

'No way!' said the thick. '*My* back is in bits. I had to lug those cases down three flights and then put them into the taxi. And with all the hanging around – she kept on saying, "Don't leave me! Don't leave me!" – I'm late for my next call.'

So I had to carry them upstairs myself. And they were *all* as heavy as lead. What did she have in them? Bricks?

The only thing that cheered me up
was that I didn't have to pay for the taxi.
The King had paid. I thought it very
nice of him – until it occurred to me that
maybe he was glad to be rid of her.

When I finally got all the cases up, tea
was over and Mama Bear was going up
to help Goldilocks to unpack.

'Make your own tea,' she said airily,
'the kettle is on the boil.'

3 The Breakfast

Next morning when I came down, Mama Bear was feeding Baby Bear.

'Where's Goldilocks?' I asked.

'I told her to have a lie-in. The poor thing was worn out. All that stress.'

She came down just as I was leaving for work and Mama Bear filled her up a bowl of lovely porridge. Well, it usually is lovely but by this time it was cold.

'I *hate* cold porridge,' said Goldilocks, pushing her bowl away.

Well, whose fault was that?

'Try my breakfast,' said Mama Bear.
She's into all this health food – raw oats
and nuts and bits of dried fruit. Awful!

But Goldilocks didn't like that either.
Then she looked at Baby Bear's bowl.

'That's what I want,' she said. 'Cornflakes. We always had cornflakes for
breakfast at the Royal Palace.'

So Mama Bear filled her out a bowl.

I was stunned. Cornflakes! 'No!' I tried to say. I was thinking of the cost. It was bad enough that Baby Bear ate them but from the way our new *au pair* was wolfing them down, it was clear she was going to get through sacks of the stuff.

In fact, she gobbled up all we had and Mama Bear asked me to get her more!

Then the clock struck. Due to all the fuss I hadn't left at my usual hour. I grabbed my hat and though I cycled like mad all the way to the factory I was late.

The first time in twenty years!

'It's not like you,' reproved the nasty youth who clocks everyone in. 'Watch it!'

It was with a heavy heart that I began testing, getting my fingers stickier than usual as I tried to work faster.

What next?

When I got home there was no fire, no slippers, no supper on the table.

Mama Bear, Goldilocks and Baby Bear (still up) were watching TV.

'Did you get the cornflakes?' asked Mama Bear.

To avoid an unseemly row, I had to go round to The Smart Mart, where the motto, judging by the prices, was: 'It costs more to buy less here.' If they ever had a Special Offer (they never do) it would be: 'Get 3 for the price of 4!'

When I got home again, Goldilocks was teaching Mama Bear and Baby Bear to do the 'ladybug'. She said it was the very latest thing. To me it looked like they were just throwing their arms and legs all over the place. Any old way.

After a cold supper, Goldilocks left.

'She's going to *The Dive In* with her mates,' said Mama Bear. 'It's the *in* place.'

I had to put Baby Bear to bed.

She wasn't in until midnight so she didn't get up until noon the next day.

On Saturday, I decided to have a heart-to-heart with Mama Bear.

'This carry-on will have to stop. I've made out a list of her duties which you must enforce. Listen carefully.'

6.30 am	Rise
7.00 am	Serve breakfast
	Get Baby Bear up
7.30 am	Clear away and wash up
	Washing and ironing
9.00 am	Walk with Baby Bear....

At this point, Mama Bear cut across me. 'Save your breath. *Au pairs* mind kids and do a little light work. Like dusting...shssh, here she comes.'

You should have heard her munching and crunching her flakes, milk dribbling down her face. And she's supposed to be teaching Baby Bear manners.

As I left the kitchen, I heard her say to Mama Bear, 'You're mad to be doing all that cooking. They've lovely "fast food" at The Smart Mart.'

So instead of Mama Bear's good healthy home cooking, full of vitamins A to Z, I was served up stuff a dog would have turned up his nose at.

And if it wasn't junk food it was 'cold cuts' from the '*Cold food is HOT!*' deli.

Now Baby Bear will eat nothing else...

4 The Chairs

The next showdown was looming.

On Sunday the little biddy had taken
Baby Bear for a walk (most unwillingly,
I felt) but they had hardly been gone
before they were back.

'It's my back,' she wept. 'I can't move.'

Well, anyone could have told her that if
she spent the night jerking around doing
the ladybug she was bound to do herself
an injury, but would she listen?

She spent the day in bed but when she limped down she was still moaning.

'It's all because of my chair,' she said, 'it's agony to sit on.'

And what did she do when I got up to put a log on the fire (which isn't *my* job) but hop into mine.

My chair. The one in front of the TV and out of the way of all the draughts.

I got really mad, but do you think she would get up when I asked her? No!

Mama Bear just smiled and said, 'Let the poor child have it if she wants it.'

Baby Bear was laughing his head off to see his old man in such a rage.

Luckily she decided she didn't like my chair. Too hard. So she decided to try Mama Bear's.

But that didn't suit her either. Too soft – the springs had broken. So when Baby Bear got up to play with his train set, she nipped in, quick as a flash. A great big smile spread over her face.

'This is the one for me,' she said. 'It's so comfy. And just the right size.'

Now she was able to touch the ground with her feet instead of having to dangle them in mid-air.

When Baby Bear saw she had taken his chair, he let out a scream that could have been heard in the Royal Palace.

But Goldilocks only smirked. 'Ask your Papa to buy you a nice new chair.'

What do you think happened next?

You just won't believe it!

She began tilting the chair back and forth as she swung her legs.

Next thing there was an awful crash and the chair was in bits on the floor.

Mama Bear and I had to hold back Baby Bear as he tried to kick her.

'Serve them both right,' I thought, smiling behind my hand (which was probably not a wise thing to do).

When Mama Bear saw me smiling, she got very annoyed. With me!

'Good riddance to bad rubbish,' she growled. 'Come,' to Goldilocks, 'we'll throw out these two old chairs and take in the sofa from the parlour.'

The sofa?

The best bit of furniture in the house. Only used on special occasions.

But there they were, dragging it in and putting it in front of the fire – it was so big it took up half the room. Even Baby Bear, now all smiles, was helping.

Then they all sat down to watch TV.

My chair had been pushed away behind the sofa and as the back was so high I couldn't see a thing. As for getting any heat, I might as well have been in the Arctic circle.

I was cold and hungry...and furious.

What was Goldilocks at? I don't think she ever took Baby Bear for a walk and he was staying up later and later.

She had persuaded Mama Bear to drop cooking. Not only because Fast Foods and Cold Cuts were easier. She said I was too fat and should slim!

Me? I'm the perfect size!

Suddenly I saw red. I leaped up.

Go to your room at once!'

'Go to your room *at once*,' I shouted to Goldilocks. 'No supper tonight!'

'What's for supper?' she asked, cool as an ice-cube.

'I've got this lovely minced cow heel,' said Mama, showing us some granules. 'So easy...just add water and serve.'

'just add water'

Goldilocks pulled a face, indicating what she thought of minced cow heel.

'I think I'll pass up supper,' she said, 'I really need a good long sleep.'

But if I thought a night without supper was going to turn her into a better *au pair,* I had another think coming.

Next morning she was as sassy as ever and into the cornflakes like a locust.

Then she dropped her bombshell.

'I'm afraid I won't be able to look after Baby today,' she said casually. 'I have to go into the village. My aunt texted me last night. She's at death's door.'

As usual, Mama Bear was all deep concern and gave her the day off.

I had no time to argue as I had to dash. I didn't want to be late again.

When I got home, the little biddy was nowhere to be seen.

'She's having a rest,' said Mama Bear. 'She's very upset about her aunt.'

Later one of the Spratt boys – they're a nasty mean lot – called to the door. He had a bunch of flowers with him, no doubt nicked from the local graveyard.

'I've called for Goldilocks,' he said.

'I don't think she'll go out,' I said, 'her aunt is very poorly.'

'I think she will,' he said, taking a seat.

And of course Mama Bear was all over him, giving him cake and lemonade.

Half an hour later Goldilocks came down, dolled up to the nines.

'Super!' said Spratt junior. 'And at lunch you said you couldn't find a thing to wear....did you text the gang?'

'They're going to *The Two Left Feet*,' said Mama Bear. 'It's much smarter than *The Dive In*.'

Not a word about the poor old aunt. I wondered if she had ever existed.

When they had gone, I began to complain to Mama Bear, but she cut me off.

'You're always giving out about her. Let the poor thing enjoy her youth.'

Just then Baby Bear chipped in.

'You never got my new chair,' he said.

'Yes, what about the two new chairs?' asked Mama Bear.

I decided to go to bed early.

5 The 'Gang'

At about midnight, I woke up to the banging of cars and doors and the sound of voices. The 'gang' had arrived.

'They're all in the house,' I said to Mama Bear. 'They'll be eating our ice-cream and drinking our lemonade.'

In another two minutes that was the

least of my worries. By a long straw.

There was an explosion of noise.

And it was ear-splitting.

There seemed to be about three bands,
all playing at top pitch.

Mama Bear, eyes closed, had her ear-
plugs in and pretended not to hear.

I grabbed my dressing-gown and
rushed downstairs.

I was right. There were several music players at work, all thumping out sound.

'Stop this noise **at once**,' I shouted at Goldilocks who was ladybugging past.

'What's the problem?' she said, all big blue eyes. 'Don't you like music?'

'Don't you just dig that crazy Lean Boy Stout,' squealed Spratt junior, turning up the sound and adding a cracked voice to the uproar.

'Bet my ghetto-blaster is louder than your boom-box,' howled another creep.

Just then the phone rang. It was the Wilde-Bores, our next-doors.

'Stop that music *at once*!'

They could hardly speak with rage.

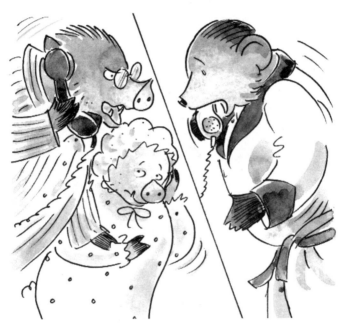

'I'm trying to,' I yelled. '*I'm* not playing it. It's some friends of our new *au pair*. She came from the Royal Palace.'

That made them even madder.

'You and your fancy babysitter. We'll soon put a stop to this carry-on.'

And before you could say 'nine, nine, nine' there was a squad car at the door and policemen were rushing in and arresting everyone in sight.

Except Goldilocks who had quietly slipped away at the first sign of trouble.

The gang were in stitches.

'I think things are going pear-shaped,' chortled Jack Spratt.

'You mean *bear*-shaped,' yelled a pal.

As if things weren't bad enough – the noise, the screams, the policemen, the neighbours in bunches outside – a little weasel from *The Daily Howl* cast up.

'Why are you being arrested?' he asked.

'I'm not being arrested,' I said, trying to break free of a policeman. 'I own the house. I'm trying to restore order.'

He licked his pencil and took out his pad. I could see what he wrote:

'Party at Papa Bear's House Gets Out of Hand. Police Called'

I froze. I could see what that would lead to. Me in court! The neighbours cutting us dead! My job under threat!

'Please don't print that,' I pleaded.

He obligingly wrote another headline:

Papa Bear Tries to Bribe Press

At this stage Mama Bear came down and had a look at the mess. Tables and chairs upended. Fridge cleaned out. Cans and ice-cream cartons everywhere.

44

But in the morning she wouldn't hear a word against Goldilocks. No way!

'It's her friends. She wasn't there when the trouble started.'

I had to admit that was so.

'Poor thing. She's had a very hard life. Her mother died and her father married again and her two ugly sisters made her do all the work. So she had to run away.'

'She's got her story wrong!' I yelled. 'That's the story of Cinderella.'

'You'll be late for work if you don't hurry,' was all she said. Coldly.

'Don't forget my chair,' called Baby Bear after me.

The way he takes the good things of life for granted! As though the world owed him a living. I'll have to sort that young hopeful out soon. Does he think money grows on trees?

6 The Beds

I had a long tiring day at work and I was really goosed at six o'clock.

Then I remembered those stupid chairs. I would have to buy them on the way home to avoid any more hassle – Goldilocks was now in on the act.

'Have you not bought those chairs yet?' she had said the night before (before the trouble started). That sofa is very bad for their backs.'

Well, between being so tired and rushing to get to The Posh Shop before it shut and not having time to put my specs on, I made a terrible mistake.

It was only when the oily sales chap started bowing and scraping and saying, 'We'll send them "Fast Mail" – they'll be home before you are,' that it hit me.

I had misread the price-tags.

The chairs cost almost twice as much as I had meant to spend on them.

What a dilemma! To change them for

cheaper chairs would be to lose face.
Everyone in the shop would be sneering
at me – 'The skinflint bear who would
only buy the cheapest chairs in the shop.'

How the Wilde-Bores would jeer!

No! The Bears are a great and ancient
family. I could not disgrace their name.
I would have to smile and pay up.

All I wanted now was to get home,
have a cup of tea and go to bed.

And what do you think I found when
I crawled into the bedroom?

Goldilocks asleep in my bed!

She told Mama Bear she couldn't sleep a wink in her own awful bed.

I had to sleep downstairs in my armchair so you can imagine how I felt in the morning. Apart from not getting a wink of sleep, I was as stiff as a poker.

I had to get off my bicycle half way to the factory and walk. So I was late again.

'This is getting to be a habit,' said the nasty youth. 'Get up earlier!'

When I got home that evening, Mama Bear asked me, very coldly I thought, what about the chairs?

So they hadn't arrived yet! So much for 'Fast Mail'. I wondered what 'Slow Mail' would be like. Ass and cart?

Supper was cold cuts (ice outside).
And Baby Bear still wasn't in bed.

'Where's Goldilocks?' I asked.

'She's very tired. Gone to bed early.'
I had a terrible thought.

'I hope she's not in my bed.'

'No, she said it was even worse than
hers, as hard as nails. She said it was no
wonder you were always in such a bad
temper, having to sleep on that.'

Knowing I would have my bed back, I was able to relax and play a few old Dickie Rock records before putting out Mr Stinkie, the cat, and going upstairs.

Was I looking forward to a good night's sleep!

When I got upstairs, Mama Bear was already there, rooted to the spot, looking at her bed. There was someone in it!

Goldilocks!

Fast asleep, golden hair on the pillow, crisps all over the place.

Mama Bear tried to wake her. No use! So she put her things on *my* bed.

'You'll have to sleep in your chair again tonight,' she said. 'I've no chair, remember? But it'll be no hardship for you – you keep saying how comfy that awful old chair is.'

So I had to sleep in my chair for a second night.

When I got to work next day (late again), I phoned The Posh Shop.

The oily clerk was 'off', they told me. No one knew anything about the chairs.

I went home with murder in my heart.

'This will have to stop,' I said to Mama Bear as soon as I got home. 'I'm putting my foot down. Where's that little biddy?'

Then I noticed Mama Bear was crying.
'What's wrong?'

'It's Goldie,' (she had taken to calling
her 'Goldie'), 'she was so tired today she
couldn't get up. I told her she could
have my bed and sleep all day. She's ill.
She needs help.'

Was she mad? Goldie was as helpless
as a rattlesnake. But Mama Bear was so
upset that all I could do was say that
I would help her, that we would both
go up to Goldilock's room to see if we
could find any clue to her tragic
illness.

Well, we found plenty.

Near the window was a basket with a rope tied to it. On the sill lay a list from *The Purple Duck Take-Away*. Empty cartons and tubs lay all over the place.

On the bed, a sight that almost made me weep, was Baby Bear's money-box. Forced open. Only a cent or two left.

It all became clear as a bell to me.

When I ordered Goldilocks to her room without supper, far from spending the evening in tears, repenting her sins, she had been having a whale of a time.

She used to text her order to *The Purple Duck*, lower the basket with *my* money in it, then haul up red-hot chilli peppers or rubber duck or whatever.

The crook!

And after a good meal she would spend the rest of the time texting the gang and setting up dates for next day.

But worse was to come. There was a half-written letter on the table beside the bed. It was to her mother.

'Dear Mum, I can't begin to tell you what this place is like. It's AWFUL. Old Bear is always moaning about something. The wife (ninety at least) thinks she's "with it" – you should see her trying to dance. And she can't cook for toffee. The meals are pure yuck. I have to live on fruit and nuts. Please take me away before I starve to death or collapse from fatigue. I can't sit in the chairs or lie on the beds. Anyway there's no time. I work from six in the morning until midnight...'

Mama Bear gave a terrible scream.

'You ungrateful little hussy,' she yelled, 'I'll...I'll...'

What she was going to do I'll never know because just then there was a loud crash from Baby Bear's room.

We rushed in to find him in tears. He pointed at Goldilocks who was lying on what was left of his bed. It was in bits.

She had left Mama Bear's bed and parked herself in Baby Bear's.

With dire results!

'Call a taxi,' shouted Mama Bear.

She grabbed Goldilocks by the scruff of the neck and dragged her downstairs.

Luckily a taxi was at the door. 'Fast Mail' had just made it with the chairs.

Goldilocks was bundled into it, hissing, 'I'll sue you for this?' and Mama Bear was yelling, 'Out! Out! Out!'

'Take her to the Palace,' I said to the taximan, 'and give them this letter.'

It was the one she had given us when she arrived. 'Tell them we couldn't steal this jewel from the Royal Nursery.'

'What about my cases?' she shrieked.

'Wait!' I told the taximan.

As I threw her cases out of the window – what a joy – I said, 'Give the King the bill, and demand a good fat tip.'

And off they rattled.

We soon had the place cleared and the two new chairs set up in the living room. Mama Bear and Baby Bear couldn't thank me enough.

'You were only thinking of us all the time,' said Mama Bear, 'and all I did was give out to you. Now you must get yourself a luxury chair just like ours.'

'We might try new beds too,' I said.

Now when I come home, the fire is blazing, supper is ready and Mama Bear and Baby Bear do all they can for me.

We are one big happy family again.

Goldilocks, the baby-sitter from hell, is just a fading memory.